This ELMER book belongs to:

. . . .

for Princess Bakhta

This paperback edition published in 2012 by Andersen Press Ltd.
First published in Great Britain in 2002 by Andersen Press Ltd.,
20 Vauxhall Bridge Road, London, SW1V 2SA, UK
Vijverlaan 48, 3062 HL Rotterdam, Nederland
Copyright © David McKee, 2002

Colour separated in Switzerland by Photolitho AG, Zürich.
Printed and bound in China.

5   7   9   10   8   6   4

British Library Cataloguing in Publication Data available.

ISBN 978 1 84270 938 2

www.elmer.co.uk

ELMER

and Butterfly

David McKee

Andersen Press

Elmer, the patchwork elephant, was out walking
when a shout came from up a tree: "Hello, Elmer."
"Is that you, Monkey?" Elmer called back.
"No, it's me," laughed cousin Wilbur from behind
a bush.
"Hello, Wilbur," chuckled Elmer. "You are clever
with your voice tricks. I'm going for a walk.
See you later."

1

Not long after that, another voice called,
    "Help! Help!"
 Elmer smiled and said, "All right, Wilbur, come on out."
The voice called again, "Help! I'm trapped." Elmer laughed.
"If that's you, Wilbur..."
But before he could finish he saw that it was Butterfly,
    trapped in a hole behind a fallen branch.

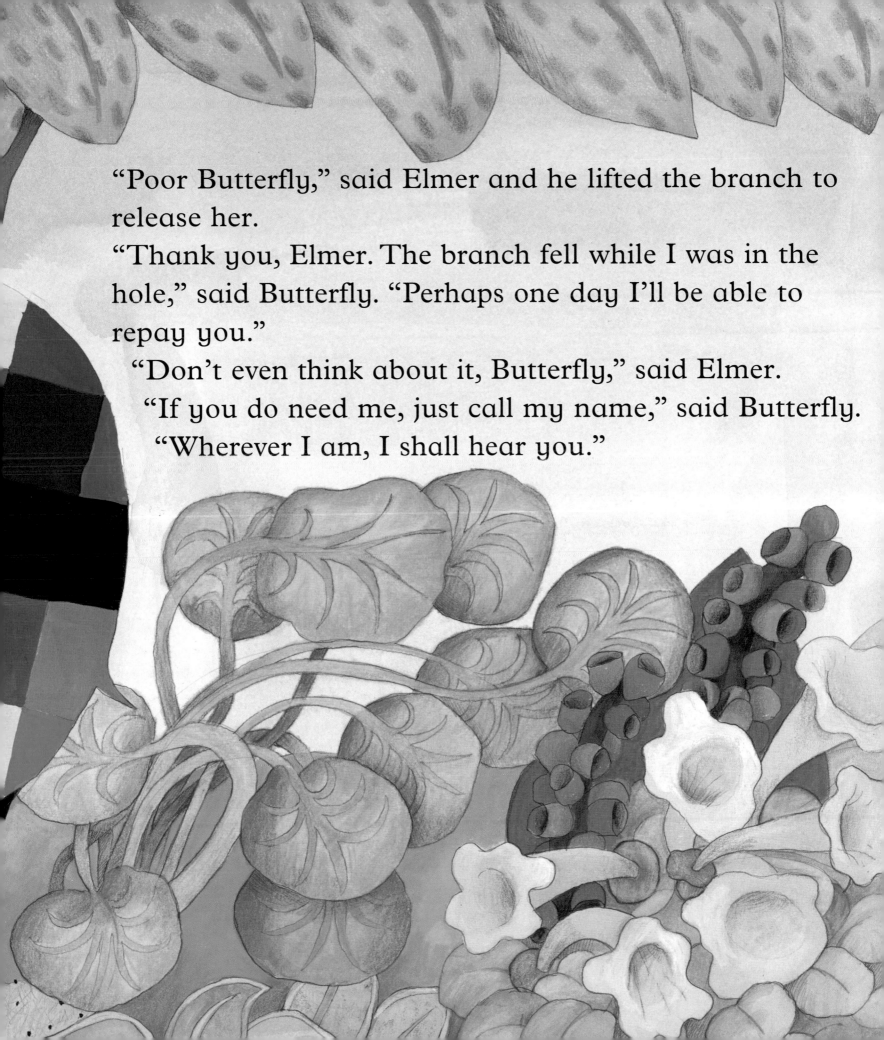

"Poor Butterfly," said Elmer and he lifted the branch to release her.

"Thank you, Elmer. The branch fell while I was in the hole," said Butterfly. "Perhaps one day I'll be able to repay you."

"Don't even think about it, Butterfly," said Elmer.

"If you do need me, just call my name," said Butterfly.

"Wherever I am, I shall hear you."

"A butterfly saving an elephant, that's a good one!"
chuckled Elmer as he continued his walk.
At that point, a narrow path led off the main one.
"I've never been here before," he said.
"This looks interesting."

The path suddenly led out of the trees and along a cliff
face high above the valley below.
"This is dangerous," said Elmer. "And the path goes to
a cave. I'll go back... Oh, dear! Going backwards here
isn't easy. I'll go to the cave, turn around and walk back
normally."

Elmer was nearly there when the path started falling.
He rushed into the cave and peeped out. Part of the
path had gone.
"Oh no! There's no way back," he said. "Help!"
he shouted. There was no answer.

"Help!" Elmer called again. Still no answer.
"They're all too far away," he thought. "I'll try Butterfly.
Butterfly! Help!" he called.
He was about to try again when Butterfly arrived.

"Oh, Butterfly, thank goodness!" said Elmer.
"Now it's me who is trapped in a hole."
"Don't worry, Elmer," said Butterfly.
"I'll get help."

Wilbur was amusing a group of elephants when Butterfly arrived. She quickly told them about Elmer. In no time the elephants were rushing to the rescue.

At the cliff top the elephants saw how dangerous it was and most kept away from the edge. Wilbur disappeared back among the trees.

One or two elephants carefully peeped over the edge
to try and spot Elmer. "I see his trunk," said one.

Wilbur soon came hurrying back, pulling
a very long, very strong creeper.
He threw one end over the edge of the cliff
and called down, "Catch hold, Elmer."

"Tie the creeper around you and hold on tightly," said Butterfly. "Don't worry. It will be all right."

Elmer tied the creeper firmly and called out, "I'm ready."
The elephants caught hold of the creeper and pulled. Elmer swung out from the cave and then upwards.

Once he was safe, Elmer thanked them all,
especially Butterfly.
"Fancy a butterfly saving an elephant!" he said.
Then a shout came from the cave, "Don't forget me."
The elephants stared. "Who else is there?" said one.
"Just Wilbur's voice," laughed Elmer. "Let's tickle him."
But Wilbur was already running home.

Read more ELMER stories!

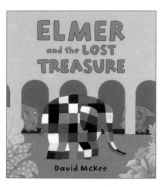

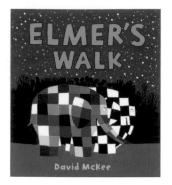

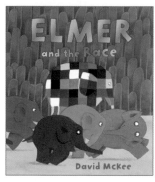

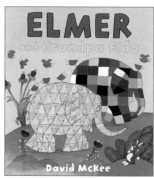

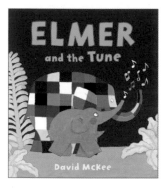

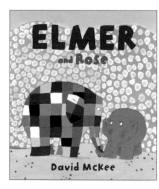

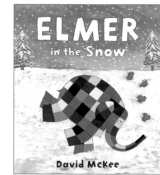

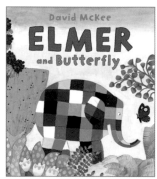

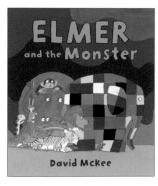

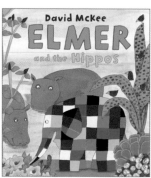

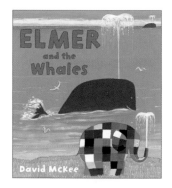

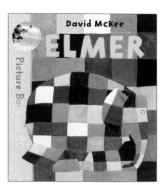

Discover all of ELMER's adventures at:
www.elmer.co.uk